For Bear
N. W.

Pour mon petit poisson
M. G.

First edition 2004

Library of Congress Cataloging-in-Publication Data

Wood, Nancy C.
Old coyote / Nancy Wood ; illustrated by Max Grafe.
p. cm.
Summary: Realizing that he has come to the end of his days,
Old Coyote recalls many of the good things about his life.
ISBN 0-7636-1544-7
[1. Coyote—Fiction. 2. Death—Fiction.] I. Grafe, Max, ill. II. Title.
PZ7.W853 Ol 2004
[E]—dc21   2002035005

2 4 6 8 10 9 7 5 3 1

Printed in Singapore

This book was typeset in Quercus.
The illustrations were done in mixed media on paper.

Candlewick Press
2067 Massachusetts Avenue
Cambridge, Massachusetts 02140

visit us at www.candlewick.com

OLD COYOTE

NANCY WOOD
ILLUSTRATED BY MAX GRAFE

CANDLEWICK PRESS
CAMBRIDGE, MASSACHUSETTS

Old Coyote was going along.

Through familiar fields he went, across a little stream whose merry song he recognized. He stopped for a drink. "Hello, Stream," he said. As he drank, he saw his reflection in the water. "I have grown old," he said.

Old Coyote was old. He was as old as coyotes get. He remembered a time when there was no city near his home. He remembered a time before the noisy and dangerous highway. He remembered a time when his howl was so loud that even the earthworms up on the mountain could hear it.

Now Old Coyote's howl was squeaky, and not so loud. His muzzle was turning white.

Old Coyote couldn't run anymore, so he walked along. He stuck his head in a rabbit hole as he passed by and shouted, "Hello, down there! It's a nice day. I plan to make the most of it." Beneath the ground, the rabbits huddled in fear. Old Coyote had eaten many of their kind before. "My days of eating rabbits are over," Old Coyote said.

After a while, Old Coyote's back felt stiff and sore. He went past a saguaro stretching its arms to the sky. "When the desert sand was hot and burned my paws, you let me borrow your shade," he said. "Thank you." The saguaro was even older than Old Coyote. It had many more years to go.

Now the sun was higher over the horizon. Old Coyote greeted it with a swish of his tail. "Father Sun," he said, "you have warmed my days. Without you, I would have been cold." He stretched his tired legs. The sun heated his back. "How beautiful the world is," he said to himself, as he turned from the desert to make his way up into the forest.

At last Old Coyote came to a large pine tree that stood guard over the den where he lived. When Old Coyote was just a young pup starting out, he had dug the tunnel all by himself, scooping out the dirt with his paws. As the years went by, the den had grown bigger and bigger.

Inside the den, Mrs. Coyote had been waiting. She gave him a coyote kiss, licking him on his face. He licked her back.

"It was a good morning," he said happily. Slowly, legs creaking, he turned around once and dropped down to the ground.

"It rained here," Mrs. Coyote said. "A rainbow stretched from here to there. The earth smelled good to me."

Old Coyote put his paw on hers and looked around. "Remember the children?" he asked. "And the grandchildren? One hundred twenty-nine in all!"

"I remember," she said. "What more could we want?"

"I'll rest for a while," Old Coyote said, looking at her tenderly. "Then I'll go."

It was the way of all coyotes. Mrs. Coyote let him curl up beside her, and while he slept, she remembered what good times they'd had. She thought about how thick Old Coyote's fur got when it snowed. She thought about him chasing a rabbit.

Then she thought about just last week, when he had stumbled. He had not caught any rabbits or squirrels for a long time. She had hunted so they could eat, while Old Coyote sat in the field with his face to the sun, enjoying the warmth.

After a while, Old Coyote stood up. He was stiff and sore, and he had forgotten where he'd left his dreams. "Ah," he said, "I know what that means."

Mrs. Coyote licked him gently on the nose. She could not speak.

Old Coyote went up to the top of the tunnel and looked out. It was a clear night, with millions of stars shining overhead. He knew them all by heart. Little bats flew past. And nighthawks. A full moon shone. "Sister Moon," he said, "light the path I have to take." And Sister Moon did just that.

When he got to a certain spot in the forest, Old Coyote stopped. Animals were gathering, as they did every full moon. Many of his old friends were there. They were in a good mood and glad to see him. "Our circle is complete," they said.

"Thank you, friends," said Old Coyote. While the others told stories, he lay down on a rock and licked his paws. They were sore from so much walking.

Old Coyote lay on his belly and watched the moon traveling across the sky. It was fat and silvery. He sat and howled at it, just the way he used to. The sound echoed all across the mountains, and the other animals complimented him. "You sound the way you did long ago," they said.

Old Coyote looked at them in the moonlight. Then he got up and shook himself. "Goodbye, my friends," he said. And he turned and climbed upward, with the wind pushing him along.

When he reached the top of the mountain, Old Coyote paused. He was very tired. He listened to the sounds around him. The cold-lipped wind. The humming insects. A little stream just beginning its watery life. The soft noise that birds make when they're going to sleep.

Old Coyote found a perfect rock. He curled up and closed his eyes. He dreamed of all his haunts and all his children. He dreamed of Mrs. Coyote's thick brown coat and fine yellow eyes. He dreamed of running through the forest with her when they were courting. He dreamed of running so fast nothing could catch him . . .

and finally, he dreamed his way into a whole new world.